Frank the Barber

Dave Dellecese

DANDY PRESS

FRANK THE BARBER

Cover Illustration by Shintayu Arifin
Based on a sketch by Megan McCoy Dellecese

Library of Congress Control Number: 2020907803

ISBN: 978-1-970156-00-3

Published by Dandy Press
Utica, New York

dandypress.com

ALSO BY DAVE DELLECESE

The Little Lamp
Lacey & Lily

*For all those who show concern for others,
especially when times are tough.*

CONTENTS

Acknowledgments

ACKNOWLEDGMENTS

Countless thanks to my wife, Megan McCoy Dellecese, who read through draft upon draft, always with a keen eye and honest critique, as well as coming up with the idea for a *Saturday Evening Post*-inspired cover.

Special thanks to John Swann, Tom Coyne, and Frank Tomaino for their endless knowledge and history, as well as the archives of the Utica Public Library, the *Utica Daily Press*, and the *Observer-Dispatch*, for helping to give this cast of fictional characters a proper place and real world in which to live.

And thank you to the late Bob Piperata, who in a random meeting in Friendly's one night, asked if I was related to a Frank the Barber, planting an unexpected seed.

CHAPTER 1

THE BARBER

Where the treetops glisten

And children listen

To hear sleigh bells in the snow

The coffee was bitter, just like the air outside. It came as no surprise to Frank. He often started his day at the Elgin Diner, and never once did his morning cup taste any better than ash from a cigar.

Some might think he was crazy for preferring it that way, but he liked things the way they were. A little consistency of his own seemed to make the chaos in the rest of the world a little easier to live with. Though how anyone could live with a world like this for much longer was anyone's guess.

Frank noticed a wrinkled mess of papers that had once been a crisp new edition of the *Daily Press* left behind at a nearby table. A cursory glance at the headlines didn't do much to make him feel any better about the state of the world.

Allied Airmen To Be Tried, Berlin Says.

Cold Wave Still Grips Area

Everything except Turkey, Butter Plentiful for Yule

Mystery Targets Under Attack Along French Shore.

He put the paper down, lacking the motivation to keep reading similar headlines. Catching up on the morning's news stories made it hard not to think about John, though deep down Frank knew he didn't need a newspaper headline to dredge up those thoughts. Every day and all day, they came. Only now, they came faster and more frequently, especially on this day of all days.

The Barber

Was this really how we're spending Christmas Eve 1943? he wondered. *Apparently.*

He sighed heavily and reached into his pocket for a few coins to pay for the coffee. It was not so long ago that Frank was craving the taste of this terrible, burnt diner coffee. Like so many others, he had gotten tired of trying to stretch that pound of coffee at home over the course of five weeks with some chicory. Fortunately, coffee had come off of the ration list over the summer. And luckily for Frank, he had always preferred his coffee black, no sweet stuff, unlike the poor entitled sap five stools down complaining loudly about the continued rationing of sugar.

The world's under siege, and you're worried about how sweet you can make your coffee? Maybe we don't deserve to win this after all.

Though it crossed his mind, he didn't say it aloud. That just wasn't Frank's style. No, sir. Frank was an observer. And now it was time to observe the sidewalk because that shop wasn't going to open on its own.

Counting out a dime, a nickel, and a few pennies for tip, Frank laid the change in front of his cup and saucer. Grabbing his hat and coat from the adjacent stool, he put them on with no real haste. He wished the staff a Merry Christmas Eve before heading out to the icy sidewalk of Lafayette Street.

The bright sun was misleading as the temperature in the city of Utica hadn't been higher than maybe 20 degrees lately. At its lowest, it had reached 20 below.

As Frank passed the Hotel Utica, a man exited and turned up his collar to combat the cold air hitting his face. In the brief moment before the door closed, Frank turned his head to glance inside, catching sight of the lobby's manger scene, along with what was probably the most beautiful wreath he'd ever seen. Barbara would have loved it.

The slick soles of Frank's shoes weren't made for slippery surfaces, and he was glad he'd spent $1.55 on galoshes at Neisner's a few years ago, even if they now squeaked annoyingly with every step. It certainly took away any element of surprise wherever he went, including to the newsstand at Columbia and Seneca Streets where Helen Hoffman was bundled up trying to stay warm beside her little shack outside the First Bank and Trust building.

"Heard you coming all the way from Lafayette Street," Helen cackled. "Time for a new pair."

"Nothin' doin'," Frank smiled. "'sides, my feet are probably worth more than my house these days."

"You ain't kiddin'," she said, pulling her weather-beaten coat and kerchief a little tighter to keep out the cold. They were never the fanciest of clothes, but what she lacked in elegance of wardrobe, Helen more than made up for in pure grit. Since the 1920s, no matter the weather, Helen could be found at her ramshackle stand selling papers, magazines and comic books. Some folks didn't even take the time to get out of their cars to grab their morning news. They just drove up to the curb and Helen brought the paper to them. Some said she'd even place a bet for you if you wanted.

One thing that was a sure bet - with the war going on, rubber like the kind on Frank's feet was scarce. Most of the world's supply came from trees in Southeast Asia. By the first few months of '42, the Japanese occupation there had America scrounging for every bit they could get. Frank had been using newspaper under his feet to make these worn out old things last just a little bit longer until the fighting was over. He had already given up to the cause everything else that could be used - a busted garden hose, his wife's old yellow scrubbing gloves, John's childhood raincoat, and the tires from the old jalopy. Sure, it limited him to where his own two feet could take him, but those boys needed all the help they could get.

Helen asked if Frank wanted to see the morning's *Daily Press*, but having already skimmed it over coffee, Frank politely passed. Instead, he turned to an assortment of colorful comic books on a shelf. One had a trio of costumed characters sitting on Santa's lap. Another had a star-spangled gal by the name of Wonder Woman lifting an entire train above her head. *Who thinks of this stuff*, Frank chuckled to himself. He then spotted one that would serve his purposes just fine: a copy of *Action Comics*. The bright yellow cover featured the blue figure of Superman using giant bobby pins to fasten some garishly dressed crooks to the wall, with an equally colorful blurb: *"Needles and pins, needles and pins, When the Prankster meets Superman, trouble begins!"*

Helen raised a skeptical eyebrow as Frank pulled the magazine off the rack and handed over a dime. Of all the crazy characters in those magazines, Frank had actually heard of this Superman character before. Frank kept a radio in his workspace and would occasionally overhear the "Man of Steel's" adventures while waiting on customers in the afternoon. Helen knew this wasn't Frank's usual type of reading material. Why anyone would pay good money for funnybooks was beyond her, but not *so* far beyond her that she'd reject the ten cents Frank was handing over.

"Benjamin says thank you," Frank told her.

That explained it. Helen smiled thinking of how Frank looks out for that kid, especially since no one else on the street would. After an impulse purchase of the *Saturday Evening Post* (the cover featuring a soldier standing tall on a white, snow-covered ground under a starry sky), Frank was on his way.

He hadn't made it but a few more steps from the newsstand when he spotted Whistlin' Jim. No melodies were coming from his lips yet, still so early in the day. Lying against the cold, gray stone exterior of the Bank and Trust building, Jim was fast asleep, his tattered clothes blending into an equally tattered blanket that slipped off his body.

Frank quietly grabbed the edge of the blanket, careful not to wake Jim, pulling it up to the old man's chin before dropping a few coins into the cup on the ground beside him. *"Merry Christmas, Jim,"* he whispered, and continued along the sidewalk.

The day was still too new and the crowds had yet to take over the sidewalk as he crossed the intersection at Columbia and Genesee streets. In the distance he spotted Officer Kelly directing traffic near Liggetts Drug Store at The Busy Corner just as he had for over two decades.

It hadn't snowed in some time, but that certainly didn't stop the bitter cold from gnawing away at any piece of exposed skin it could reach. Even Frank's mustache felt like it had icicles forming at the bottom of its bristles. At times, the icy wind made it difficult to even move one foot in front of the other, but he kept at it anyway. Not much farther now.

That's when he spotted Benjamin, huddled next to his shoeshine box, teeth chattering and his lips turning blue.

"M-m-m-mornin', Frank!" the boy managed to sputter with as much enthusiasm as if it were the middle of July.

"How's business today, Ben?" Frank asked, tilting his head down to try and keep some of the cold air out of his face, though it didn't do much good.

Ben was a dedicated businessman, that was for sure. There wasn't a guy downtown who would be out looking for a shine on a morning like this, yet there he was, frozen fingertips clinging to his shine box, just in case clientele appeared.

"Business seems a little slow," Frank told him.

"C-c-c-can change in a heartbeat, Frank. Yessiree, I'll bet any minute now, they're gonna be linin' the s-s-street waitin' for a shine for all them Christmas Eve parties. J-j-just you wait. Just you wait!"

Frank could tell that Benjamin's dedication, even in this frigid weather, was a matter of pride and this wasn't going to be an easily won negotiation.

"Maybe you could just help me open up the shop?" Frank offered. "If we see a customer, I promise you're free to go." A small smile curled on Frank's face as he spun his tale of woe a little more. "I'm gettin' older, you know. I need all the help I can get."

Frank extended his right hand, offering up the copy of *Action Comics* he bought just moments earlier. Ben hemmed and hawed a bit before finally giving in to his friend.

"Awright. J-j-just for a b-b-b-it."

The lights of the barber shop flickered on slowly, bringing a yellowish tint to everything they touched. Benjamin sat by the radiator, warming himself and barely flinching at every loud clang that erupted from its metal accordion shape.

A slow, drawn out *swish* casually sounded through the shop as the bristles of Frank's broom swept across the floor, whisking away any stray hairs in its path. There wasn't much to sweep into the dustbin before the business day started, nothing like the piles of clippings Frank would be cleaning off the floor by day's end. But he liked to keep the shop as tidy as he kept the bristles of his own mustache - neat, trim, and clean. The same went for his tools of the trade; each comb banged against the counter to dislodge its few hairs, then a quick rinse in the sink.

That's when he noticed some dust had gathered on Barbara and John's photos. The frames weren't much, but the pictures inside spoke a thousand words across different lifetimes. Frank wiped the glass and the edges of the frames, starting with John's photo, admiring how handsome his son looked in his uniform. Glancing at the floor, he sighed. If he didn't keep moving, he'd be standing there all day. He put the photo back in its place of reverence, in front of the mirror and next to a snapshot of four-year-old John in knickers and suit coat.

With Barbara, he had made his peace and moved on as best he could. It was not knowing about John—the inability to mourn—that made for constant unrest.

They both sat there, encased and frozen in time, just as they were in Frank's memories. Barbara forever smiling, the black-and-white portrait didn't do her beautiful auburn locks justice. But her radiant smile was just as it was on their wedding day, when she held a handful of Lily of the Valley as she walked down the aisle. It was that same smile that had accompanied Frank on a hundred walks through the park, every family trip to the ocean, and was the only thing to bring him back down to Earth when little John drew on the bedroom walls.

She had loved this time of year.

Frank reached over to the brown, rectangular radio on a table nearby, playing around with its knobs until he was able to cut down most of the static and hear Glenn Miller's Orchestra playing "That Old Black Magic." He hummed along, tapping his foot.

With a closed-lip smile across his face, he surveyed the shop like a proud papa. For a brief moment, all was as it should be, at least here, in Frank's little corner of the world. He walked to the front window and turned on the pole out front, its red, white and blue stripes swirling, signifying the start of another day. These days, though, it was a symbol of something more. Why they were here, what was on the line.

"Keep 'em flying, boys!"

The words practically screamed from the poster in the front window of the shop, the blue lettering just below a beautiful image of planes flying through cloud-filled skies, the Stars and Stripes waving proudly behind them. Frank left the poster exactly where it was, reaching just beyond it to turn the small cardboard sign around so that anyone passing by could clearly see the word: *OPEN*.

CHAPTER 2

THE SHOESHINE BOY

It broke his little heart
When he found Santa hadn't come.
In the street he envies all those lucky boys,
Then wanders home to last year's broken toys.

Compared to the frigid cold of the sidewalk, the black-and-white checkered floor of Frank's shop was a welcome relief, even if it was almost the same temperature as the pavement outside. On a day like today, a grizzly bear might have trouble keeping itself warm under a mountain of fur.

At Frank's urging, Ben relocated from a spot between dirty towels in a basket and clean linens in a cabinet to the wooden bench next to one of the shop windows. He tried to do his part to help Frank's morning routine, tidying up a mess of magazines that had found their way under the bench.

From where Ben sat, numerous colored bottles of lotions and solutions made for a rainbow of glass on top of the white granite countertops. In the mirrors behind them, Ben could see half of the pole outside, its red, white and blue stripes swirling around and around. It was a sight that often gave him a sense of relief, salvation and sanctuary when neighborhood bullies came knocking over his shoeshine box.

The lights in the shop were starting to glow brighter, and Ben wondered how men could afford to pay for a shave as often as some around town did. Of course, he didn't know for sure how much Frank charged for a shave, or anything else. Not really. Frank had never once charged him for a haircut. When Ben pressed Frank on the matter some time ago—Ben had his pride, after all— Frank agreed to an exchange of services: haircuts for shoeshines. And the boy made sure Frank's shoes shined like the fighter planes he would see cruising through the blue skies in magazines.

With a series of *kerchunks* and *clangs* the radiator kicked into gear, its heat filling Ben with a warmth he

16

hadn't known for some time. At home, he and two siblings shared a single blanket to ward off winter's bite. Since most of the time his younger brother and sister struggled for their share of the torn piece of flannel, Ben had just gotten used to the cold. It made him enjoy all the more a warm haven on such an abominable day, even though he felt a twinge of guilt thinking of any business he might be missing as he sat there clutching the latest four-color adventure of Superman.

As Ben cherished the heat, Frank's broom danced across the floor in pursuit of stray hairs, the sound of its swishing like the start of a musical composition. Ben watched Frank's methodical cleaning routine, from the floor, then on to his tools, to the sink, even making sure the photos on his countertop were as clean as could be.

The Song Spinners rang through the air from the radio, and Ben could swear that Frank was humming along with "Comin' in on a Wing and a Prayer." Ben couldn't help tapping his foot along too, turning his attention back and forth between Frank and *Action Comics*.

This Superman guy was all right in Ben's book, standing up for the little guy, for what's right, no matter who you were. Criminals, crooked politicians, or Krauts on the fighting lines were no match for this guy. Ben wished there were more folks like that in real life to look up to, to rely on - people who didn't care how much money he did (or didn't) have, where he lived or went to church, what color his skin was.

Ben glanced up from his comic book to see that Frank had finished his cleaning and was looking at the pictures on the workstation. For a moment, he wondered if there had been any word on John, but it just didn't feel right to ask. Frank had been kind enough not only to offer some shelter but a reprieve from reality with his comic magazine gift, so why sour the mood? Though Ben couldn't understand why a guy would keep looking at photos of people he never wanted to talk about.

"Where'd ya get that shiner?" Frank called out as he sauntered across the room. The pale light of the overcast day coming in through the front window mixed with the buzzing shop lights above lit the swollen purple bruise against the dark skin of Ben's left cheek, a newly added feature he'd done his best to hide so far this morning.

"Eh, don't worry about it," Ben said. "It's nothin'."

That clearly wasn't a good enough answer for Frank, who was slowly making his way across the shop, with a stride that always seemed to lack urgency. He dropped to one knee, gently moving Ben's head to get a better look.

"Doesn't look like nothin' to me."

Before Ben could reply, he noticed that Frank was no longer staring at him, but past him, out the window. Turning, Ben saw exactly what Frank did - Miller and Butch. The pair of juvenile delinquents were on the sidewalk, looking in at Ben with their brows furrowed, their faces a mixture of disdain and menace.

Butch seemed to be mouthing something, but it was hard to hear through the window and the radio, which was now spouting "Pistol Packin' Mama." The song seemed somewhat appropriate as Frank rolled up his sleeves to meet the gaze of the two bullies outside the shop. Two kids who couldn't have been in their teens staring down a boy—and now a man five or six times their age as well.

"Don't worry about it, Frank," Ben said, trying to diffuse the situation.

"Oh, I do," Frank responded as he made his way closer to the front door. "You *have* to, Ben. If you don't worry about stuff like this, those idiots are gonna keep thinking it's okay. No, I worry about it. I've cut the hair of those two creeps since they were pups. And if they think they're gonna terrorize the folks in *this* neighborhood…"

It was the first time someone who looks like Frank had told Ben he was worth just as much as any other kid on the block.

Ben hoped that there was some way he could just slip out of the shop and go about his day avoiding this altogether. After all, folks were going to be headed to work any time now — a prime time for shoe shining, if they could stand the temperatures. The thought of Ben out there roving downtown with his shoeshine box in this cold made Frank look upon the young boy as perhaps the hardiest Utican of them all. To Ben, frozen fingers were worth it, or else he'd lose customers, and more important, lose money. And a meal on the table meant more than principle any way. It wouldn't do his mother or sisters any good to come home with nothing. Of course, none of that mattered to Miller and Butch, still lingering by the windows like ghouls on Halloween.

"HEY!"

Frank's voice cut through the boys' conversation, and both froze, knowing it was meant for them. The two turned to see Frank standing in the entrance, his back propping the door open as the pole continued its silent swirl of red, white, and blue. With no window separating them anymore, Miller and Butch were less apt to meet Frank's stare with their arrogance and their eyes dropped to the ground.

"Get in here, boys," Frank ordered.

The two bullies remained frozen, unsure of what to do, though their instincts were telling them to flee. There was no time and no chance of that happening, and though he was much older than them, Miller and Butch saw in Frank's furious eyes that they'd never make it to the newsstand. And Frank was growing impatient.

"NOW," the barber said firmer.

Fast as lightning, the two boys stumbled into the barber shop and took seats in the corner often used by waiting customers.

"Now, what seems to be the problem, gentlemen?" Frank inquired.

"Aw, get off it, Frank!" Butch responded with an audacity that was not all that surprising. It was met with the steely gaze of a man who had dealt with far greater threats than this adolescent. Backpedaling, Butch snatched off his cap, twisting it in his hands and exposing a plump head. "Er...sir."

Miller, usually second fiddle to Butch's neighborhood mischief, decided to take a stab at making their case. "It ain't nothin' to worry about! We just told him to get back to his own people. We don't need him here when they got their own neighborhoods and places. Why come here?"

"Why *not* come here?" Frank asked.

Butch chimed in with equally poor success.

"Well...well, we just wanted to make sure he understood he don't belong here, that's all. Cuz...Cuz..."

"Because you think you're better than him?" Frank asked, his chin resting in one hand while the other hand sat beneath his arm. "I can think of somebody else who thinks like that. A fella named Hitler who decided he needed to show folks who belonged and who didn't, who was superior and who was inferior. We've got thousands of boys, not much older than you, all colors, shapes and sizes, overseas right now fighting that same way of thinking."

Butch's cap could not have gotten any tighter in his grip. "Well, gee, we didn't think…"

Frank cut him off abruptly. "No, you didn't. I've been cutting the hair on both your heads since you were old enough to walk. And underneath that hair, I know you've both got brains in there…somewhere. Start using them. We're fighting a war for America. Benjamin's as American as you or me so don't tell me otherwise. And also…he's my friend. So, if you've got a problem with my friend, let's hear it."

Both boys looked down at the floor.

"Gosh, we're sorry," Miller said.

Butch quickly chimed in as well. "Yeah, we ain't no Hitler."

Frank stared at them both.

"Now, go. I'll see you both next Sunday for your haircut. I don't want to find out from anybody—and I mean *anybody*—that you're back at it again, with Benjamin or anyone else. You got me?"

The boys nodded as they made their way out the door, turning to Ben before it closed. "We're, uh...we're sorry, Ben."

Ben said nothing, but nodded, unsure how long this armistice would last. But he was grateful for the moment.

As Miller and Butch sheepishly moved past the window out of sight, Frank sighed.

"I'm sorry," he said, lowering himself into one of the customer chairs. "I didn't mean to fight your battle for you, Ben. But those boys just really burned me up."

He looked at the postcards tacked to the wall, messages from around the world as he continued.

"We all come from somewhere. What the hell makes us any different from the next guy?"

Another heavy sigh. Frank wasn't sure what to say, and neither was Ben, but maybe the silence was just what they needed.

"Better get back to work," Frank said, standing up again. "Probably got a line of customers waiting for you. Who wants to spend Christmas Eve with dirty shoes?"

As Ben walked out, he turned to Frank, put a thumb and finger to his worn, tattered cap, and tipped it with a shy smile.

CHAPTER 3

THE LAWMAN

Hear them all cheering,
Now they are nearing,
There's the captain stiff as starch.
Bayonets flashing,
Music is crashing,
As the wooden soldiers march.

There was still a distinct bite to the clinging cold as early morning turned to day and the streets became busier. The shoeshine boy pulled his jacket up around his neck as he passed several storefronts. His head immediately looked downward as he passed the cop on the beat.

Officer O'Malley turned his head, eyebrows arched, even as he continued in the opposite direction. He thought about following the boy, or even stopping him, but the shiver down his spine reminded O'Malley how much the movement of walking his beat kept him warm when it was so unbearably cold. He adjusted his black scarf, making sure his neck was well insulated, and carried on.

"Morning, O'Malley!" came a hoarse shout from across the street.

It was Bruno, hurrying along with a crate of food from Chanatry's, no doubt getting ready for the Christmas Eve crowd at the restaurant. O'Malley smiled and offered a wave as he cheerfully continued along his daily path.

"Officer…"

The soft voice came with a beautiful smile to match. As the young woman approached, O'Malley simultaneously reached up to touch the brim of his cap – and slipped on an icy patch. He was grateful he didn't fall flat, but the artless way he regained his footing would have made Fred Astaire cringe - his big toothy grin outdone only by his cartoonishly wide eyes and even wider jutting jawline.

"Ma'am," he said gently as the young woman passed by, her hands to her mouth, covering a giggle.

His dignity somewhat restored, O'Malley continued, glancing around to see if anyone had noticed his literal slip-up. But no one else saw.

With nightstick at his side, he resumed his jaunty walk past the Boston Store, The Oneida National Bank and Trust Company and then Daw's Drugs, giving a small salute across the street to Officer Kelly who was helping an older woman through the intersection under the neon glow of Liggetts Drugstore. Continuing another block or two, O'Malley decided to see what was shaking over at Helen's newsstand. The bitter cold put no damper on the young officer's showmanship, waving to more passersby and whistling "Oh, What a Beautiful Mornin'" until a member of the audience turned on the star performer.

"Hey! Bing Crosby!" a gravelly voice shouted with little concern for courtesy or volume.

O'Malley stopped, looking around to see if there was anybody else Mr. Flanagan could be shouting at. The confusion must have been evident on his face, as it only made Flanagan angrier. With a frustrated face the perfect shade of tomato, Flanagan looked about ready to throw a tantrum like a toddler in a three-piece suit on the bank steps.

"Yes, you, ya big lummox!"

O'Malley stepped off the sidewalk and narrowly avoided an Oldsmobile coming his way. The driver delivered several choice words that outdid Flanagan's in both color and variety. O'Malley waved an apology as he hurried across the street to the infuriated Flanagan.

"Gee, Mr. Flanagan, you all right?"

"Am I alright? Am I alright?" his voice grew louder each time. "I come down here to make a deposit of my hard-earned money and this bum is out in front of the bank like it's a damn hotel!"

O'Malley looked to the sidewalk only to see old Whistlin' Jim, with his back against the stone wall of the First Bank and Trust Company. Jim seemed half in the world and half out of it. His tattered clothes and ragged blanket were more appropriate for a scarecrow standing guard at a farm field in the valley, a stark contrast to the Arrow collars and Mehringer sport coats he had worn a lifetime ago.

O'Malley's upper lip turned downward in an expression of pity, pleading for a little sympathy from the complainant.

"Aw, come now, Mr. Flanagan. Whistlin' Jim ain't hurtin' anybody."

"I didn't ask ya for yer assessment of the situation. I asked ya to do yer damn job. Now get him out of here before I call yer sergeant! Or maybe you'd like me to go right to Mayor Corrou!"

"Gosh, Mr. Flanagan. You know Corrou's only mayor for another week."

A guttural growl rose up as if from the very bottom of Flanagan's feet and would have given a grizzly bear pause, much less a young patrolman.

"Okay, okay!" O'Malley acquiesced. "No need to get sour about it, Mr. Flanagan. I'll take care of it."

The door to the cavernous interior of the Bank and Trust slammed behind Flanagan like a crash of thunder on a hot summer night.

Crouching down, O'Malley carefully slipped his right arm around Jim's back, his hand grasping the frail form of the old man's once sturdy chest. As Jim slowly stood up, the movement was enough to shake off whatever sleep remained. O'Malley could tell from the wide, weathered eyes and lost look within them that Jim was unsure, even a little terrified, of what was happening. By the time both were upright, the fog had visibly lifted from Jim's mind as his eyes grew narrowly suspicious.

"Come on, Jim," the officer said as quietly as he could. "We gotta move."

Jim was having none of it. "Get off me, ya big palooka!"

Although the years of hunger and heartache had taken their toll, Jim still had enough strength to send the officer stumbling backward. O'Malley's feet flew out from beneath his massive torso, flailing as he waved his arms clumsily in an attempt to regain any semblance of balance. It was as if his department-issued black boots had stepped right onto an oil slick, with all traction lost as his feet slid back and forth on the cold, hard surface below. Like two cyclones spinning in circles, his arms moved faster and faster to no avail, his feet flying up into the air; his body plummeting rear-first onto the icy sidewalk, then sliding into a nearby lamppost.

"Well, gee whiz, Jim. That's no way to say thank you," said O'Malley as he picked himself off the ground yet again. "I'm just tryin' to help ya move."

Jim sighed. "Where would ya like me to go, Sidney?"

"Aw, c'mon, Jim. Don't be like that. You know I don't wanna do that. But if I do nothing and he calls my captain then we're both in trouble and they'll make ya move anyway."

An audible scoff came from the old man as he looked away, clutching the hole-ridden rags he called clothes closer to his gaunt frame. The rebuff was palpable, and O'Malley looked all around him, into the air and down to the ground for a solution that failed to present itself.

"Look, how's about ya walk with me along my beat and we'll find ya a spot with less sourpusses?"

"Aw, all right. I'll walk with ya," Jim said gruffly. "As long as ya quit yer yappin'."

Officer O'Malley's relieved toothy grin lit up his burly, boyish face. Putting one foot in front of the other, the duo set off. The company must have lightened Jim's disposition a bit, as it took only one block before he was whistling "Pennies from Heaven" with the blue and gold-clad policeman beside him swaying his head left and right to the tune. So caught up was he in their traveling musical that at one-point Jim seemed lighter than air, dancing along the sidewalk to the delight of passersby, proving he could still cut a rug with the best of them. It took only one more block before O'Malley started getting chatty again.

"Having to tell folks like yourself to move is the kind of stuff I hate about the job, y'know? I like talking to people, though. It's great. See everyone in the neighborhood, keep an eye on things, but come on, you're not hurtin' anybody."

"You wear the uniform, though, Sidney. Comes with the territory."

"Not the uniform I wanna be wearin' right now, Jim. You know that."

"I know," Jim quietly replied, keeping his gaze forward as they continued to walk, a bit slower now.

"Look at me!" O'Malley shouted, puffing out his chest and presenting his arms. "A perfect specimen on all counts! All except this damn hernia."

The conversation paused as O'Malley, night stick in hand, touched the brim of his hat with an eye toward the girl from the counter at The Boston Store. His grin followed his gaze as she smiled back and went on her way in the opposite direction. As she walked away O'Malley still stared, perhaps in the hope she would turn around.

"Wowee. Now why can't I find a nice girl like that, Jim?"

The old man's mouth turned upward into a sly smile. "Have you tried maybe listening instead of just talking all the time?"

O'Malley turned with a confused look on his face. "Huh?"

"Nothing, Sidney. Nothing."

As they made their way around the corner, O'Malley looked skyward like a basset hound seeking the answer he was looking for.

"Now what was I sayin'? Oh yeah. It just ain't right, Jim. Seems like everybody's overseas doin' their part. Y'know, John Phelan just enlisted. Heads out for active duty in January. Heck, nearly anybody my age in the department's over there stickin' it to Hitler and his Nazis!"

His voice began to drift.

"But not me."

"You're doing your duty, Sidney. It's all any of us can do."

"My duty? Pfh! There's guys out there savin' the world, Jim! And I'm just walkin' here."

They continued, neither saying a word, even as they passed four girls that in any other moment would have turned O'Malley's head. But right now, he didn't care about anything other than an elusive dream.

"It's no wonder no girl wants to settle down with a maroon like me. Don't get me wrong. I try to make the best of it, Jim. I put on the uniform every morning. I get down to the station, surrounded by a bunch of guys too old to ship out. I put on the smile, gab on the sidewalks. But I know what the deal is. Other guys are sending postcards back home, Jim. Real-life heroes! Sending postcards home...where failures like me are waitin.'"

"Just because you failed to serve doesn't make you a failure, Sidney. If you look around you, you'd see just how much of a success you are. That little card with the 4-F on it may not be what you wanted but look around ya. Tommy Riley's just turned eight years old."

"He's growin' up fast."

"He wouldn't be growin' up at all if you hadn't pulled him out of the way of that ice truck when he was two, now would he?" Jim asked.

O'Malley said nothing. It might have been a first for him, Jim thought, before continuing. "And Mrs. Lansing. Would she be here to take care of those children at the orphanage if you hadn't pulled her out the smoke of her old apartment?"

"I never really thought about it that way, Jim."

"Nobody sees what's right in front of 'em every day when you're too busy lookin' off to the distance," Jim replied. "You may be lookin' in the mirror and seein' a failure, but these folks...you're no failure to them. You're a hero! Right here at home where they need him the most."

Jim's voice was raspy, but his clear blue eyes stared straight into the officer's soul.

The silence that followed made their steps along the sidewalk seem like the only sound in the whole city until they reached Frank's Barber Shop.

"Just goin' for a snip," O'Malley said, motioning to the shop door. "But yer welcome to join! Y'know Frank'd love to see ya."

Jim's knees were already bent as the old man eased himself into a new spot underneath Frank's front window. "I'm sure he would. But my weary old bones need a rest."

O'Malley unwrapped his scarf and handed it to the old man. "Here, now. If you're gonna be stubborn, at least be stubborn and warm all at once."

Jim smiled. And as he stood with one hand on the shop's front door, O'Malley smiled too. It was a closed mouth smile that showed more thoughts running through his head than the young police officer could ever express. So, he mustered up the only words he could.

"Thanks, Jim."

"Thank YOU, officer."

CHAPTER 4

THE VAGABOND

Silent Night
Holy Night
All is calm
All is bright

All was black. There was a feeling of still nothingness and absolute calm.

That is, until something shakes the world, and the piercing light breaks through.

Jim began to wake as a feeling of flight rushed through him. He was moving upward, but through no action of his own. His mind tried to puzzle together what was happening. Had the cold finally done him in? Was he leaving this earthly realm, bound for the pearly gates?

Seeing the long arm of the law wrapped around his midsection brought him back to reality. It was that nincompoop in the blue uniform, O'Malley.

The big lunkhead was saying something about moving, but the words weren't all that clear to Jim, who was still shaking off the daze of slumber that left him out of sync with the reality around him. Instinct took over and Jim pushed out his gangly arms. He apparently still had enough strength to knock O'Malley backward onto the sidewalk and into a nearby lamppost.

Jim couldn't help but laugh at the sight of the big lug taking a fall.

"Well, gee whiz, Jim. That's no way to say thank you," the officer said as he pulled himself up off the ground. "I'm just tryin' to help ya move."

Jim sighed. "Where would ya like me to go, Sidney?"

"Aw, c'mon, Jim. Don't be like that. You know I don't wanna do that. But if I do nothing and he calls my captain, then we're both in trouble and they'll make ya move anyway."

It must have been Flanagan; Jim knew there were few others who would make so much trouble about where he chose to hang his proverbial hat on any given day. No sense in fighting with O'Malley about it, though. It wasn't the officer's fault that Flanagan was such a snob. The old man thought about heading north, back to the bridge where McCoy was likely to still be sitting near a fire sipping on hooch, but something about the cold, fresh air smelled good. Jim took in a big whiff of it. It's not as though he hadn't been breathing it in every day, but for a moment, it just seemed more refreshing than normal.

O'Malley smiled like the big ol' wide-eyed Boy Scout he was, proud of pleading his case that had convinced a grumpy old man to keep him company on the frozen streets of the city. As refreshing as the air was, it did little to make Jim forget the frigid temperatures as they walked along.

Feeling energized and with a spring in his step, Jim put his lips together and began whistling "Pennies from Heaven." He could see the skeptical look on O'Malley's face.

"Ya think you know everything, don't ya?!" Jim's gravelly voice shouted mockingly at the officer, intending a joke, but seeming more like a vagabond's crazy rantings to those they passed. "Well, I used to be a regular Nijinsky, ya know!"

Jim's feet practically levitated as he executed a medley of moves that combined the Charleston, foxtrot, and somehow even the tango into an amalgam of movement that drew a round of surprised applause from those nearby. His long, ragged coat flowed like a flag on a ship's mast as Jim took a melodramatic bow, soaking in the laughter, smiles, and claps from the passersby. Out of the corner of his eye he could see O'Malley blushing from the attention.

They had only walked a block or so more when O'Malley started to fall back into his usual pattern of chattiness, apologizing and saying how much he hated the parts of his job that make him tell folks like Jim to move on. Jim was used to it and told O'Malley as much. It was the officer's job, after all.

As O'Malley spoke about his distaste for remaining home while so many others were off on the front lines, Jim's mind drifted a bit. For many, it was hard not to look back longingly on life before the war, but for Jim, life was pretty much the same as it had been before. Only now those around him shared the same sense of uncertainty that he had already been feeling for so many years. He wasn't ignorant of what was happening in the world, catching up on events from street conversations and days-old newspapers that also served as personal insulation under his coat.

Yes, life (if you could call this living) hadn't changed much for old Whistlin' Jim.

When he allowed himself time to reflect, it seemed like another lifetime altogether since he had earned that moniker; one that had nothing to do with the musical vagabond people of the past decade had come to know. He was a long way now from the man who lived in the nice house over on the south side of town, the man who whistled a jaunty tune whenever the ticker tape showed how much his fortunes had multiplied. Another party, a dapper hat, a new automobile – it was the norm then. So much luxury was the standard.

Until 1929.

When he was in the trenches 12 years before the crash, Jim thought the world was coming to an end. Little did he suspect the ten years that followed were not a light at the end of a tunnel but a reprieve, a delightful purgatory of glitter, riches and gaiety. No, the war to end all wars wasn't the end. Not for Jim, not for many. The world came crashing down for him on Black Tuesday and caused a series of dominoes to fall that ruined men far greater than he for a dozen years to follow.

He had been a fool but only realized it in hindsight. And he wasn't alone. Like so many others, Jim was convinced the market would keep rising forever, that times would continue to roar. A few people had warned the country that a crash was coming, but who wanted to listen? Certainly not Whistlin' Jim. Life was too good. A wonderful blur of champagne nights and social days spending what seemed like bottomless coffers of his family fortune. Even when the London Exchange followed with a fall of its own, Jim stayed optimistic that this, too, would pass. Hubris or ignorance? To this day, Jim still wasn't sure, but it didn't matter. It was all over. Gone were the parties, the women, the bubbly, and the nice house.

The large rooms dripping with crystal chandeliers, the fancy furniture, the cushioned, imported rugs were all replaced by less fashionable lodgings: an unoccupied alleyway where he could find it, with newspaper sheets and the howls of dogs from the tenements to lull him to sleep. The only woman who paid him much attention after his fall from grace was old Winifred Adams, the teetotaler with a face like a crabapple that had spent too much time rotting with the worms—and a voice to match. She and her army of charitable do-gooders would try to get him to his feet with the lure of hot soup and a shave.

"James Walter Washburn, come on, get up," he could still hear the old spinster crying out. He should have been more grateful. He realized it only in retrospect, especially as the harsh, cold winds blew through his bones on this Christmas Eve, but back then it amused him to relish in his own decline. *"Madam, I do believe I've got it made,"* he would smile, a half-full bottle of wine in his right hand, and a sly smile on his lips.

Yes, he should have been nicer to them. Over time, people looking to help folks like him didn't come around that often, if at all. Pride, that's what it was. Too proud to admit defeat, to come face to face with the idea that he really had hit the bottom.

Things looked like they might turn around in '32 when he took to the streets with his fellow veterans, marching on Washington to collect their bonus early. Who had the luxury of waiting years for their money when people were starving on the streets that very day? But it turned out to be futile. Hoover and Congress had doomed them all. Jim, like so many others, was driven out of the city by Patton and his troops, the modern-day Army versus the veterans, played out on the battlefield of D.C.'s streets.

For a time after the march, Jim thought about staying in D.C., but it was no use. He longed for home too much, even if home was just a shack in a Shantytown, a pile of hay in Brown's barn or the simple, irritating discomfort of a newspaper blanket under the bridge. It was the sights and sounds of the city that were still his, no matter what station in life he occupied. The lights along the streets twinkling like stars, the smell of roasted chickens and simmering tomato sauce on Sunday as he walked by the city's east side, or the simple smile and greeting from those he came to know day in and day out, even if they likely didn't give him a second thought.

So, a few boxcars and a lowly thumb along the road got his tired feet and whiskered chin back to the city of Utica where his heart still felt most connected.

Sure, the war had changed things. Jim saw fewer people around him on the streets, the number of vagrants dropping as more and more folks got off the curb and into jobs at the factory or even signing up for the service.

But not Jim.

He was too broken down and tired to go to work on an assembly line and too old for the military. So, the life he knew would be the life he led. At his age, he had pretty much accepted it as an absolute.

So here he was, walking these same streets once again, only now his thoughts were interrupted by the sound of O'Malley's constant prattling. For a brief moment it was as if the clouds themselves had parted and, like a gift from above, O'Malley was at a loss for words. The officer had found himself tongue tied as a young woman smiled on her way to work the counter at the Boston Store. O'Malley looked like he had been touched by an angel, smiling back at her as she passed by this odd-looking duo of beat cop and bum.

"Wowee. Now why can't I find a nice girl like that, Jim?"

The droopy, stubbled skin of Jim's chin stretched as he smiled, offering a bit of friendly advice to the lovelorn officer.

"Have you tried listening instead of just talking all the time?"

O'Malley turned with a confused look on his face, his mouth agape not unlike a gorilla's.

"Huh?"

"Nothing, Sidney. Nothing," said Jim, still smiling as he shook his head, trying hard not to chuckle.

Before long, O'Malley's continued brooding about the burden of being unfit to serve in the war along his lifelong pals brought them another block further along the officer's beat. On the other side of the world, far away from their innocent days of malteds at Kewpee's and basketball games with O'Malley, those boys were giving their all so that folks like Jim and O'Malley could walk the street as they pleased. Jim knew it tore the boy up inside to be left behind. He could see it on the officer's face, the distance in his eyes when he spoke, and his obliviousness to four more girls passing them by that in any other circumstance would have sent O'Malley into orbit.

Jim knew better than most that despair can be a powerful enemy but he also knew it was possible to make it to shore if you accept things for what they are. Once the tide comes, anything written in the sand is gone, but you can take a look around and appreciate what remains. It's what had kept him not only alive after the Crash of 1929, but vibrant. While others around him had sunk deeper into the abyss of their loss and their minds, Jim had found a way to take the events of his life and leave them where they were; with a focus, often but not always, on what was happening in the moment. Many who passed him on the street each day saw a vagabond beyond hope, but a few who got to know him learned that the stubborn curmudgeon in the tattered clothes was not as lost as some people thought.

An icy breeze blew as the two continued their sidewalk journey. Jim bit his lower lip as he thought for a moment before speaking.

"Just because you failed to serve doesn't make you a failure, Sidney. If you look around you, you'd see just how much of a success you are. That little card with the 4-F on it may not be what you wanted but look around ya. Tommy Riley's just turned eight years old."

Jim knew that Tommy wouldn't have made it to eight if O'Malley hadn't pulled him out of the way from the runaway ice truck back in '37.

When O'Malley fell silent, Jim realized he may have been the first person on Earth to get the big dolt to be quiet for a moment. Perhaps he was onto something. He looked around the neighborhood and pointed to a passing Mrs. Lansing, running errands for the orphanage. Those orphans wouldn't have her and all her good works to depend on if O'Malley hadn't pulled her from the fire at her old apartment. Here he was, berating himself as a failure, when people like them, people like Jim, owed a debt to his kindness every day.

"We rarely look at the world around us when we've got our eyes set on something in the distance, Sidney. The man you berate every day in the mirror is certainly no failure to them. He's a hero. Right here at home. Right where they need him the most."

Their steps seemed to be the only sound in the city for several moments as the men walked through the streets. The silence sank in heavier until they reached Frank's barber shop. O'Malley asked Jim to join him inside, but Jim declined, already settling down under the shop's front window. He told the officer his weary old bones needed a rest, but he wasn't about to tell him the truth. If he dared to set foot inside that shop, he'd spend the rest of Christmas Eve arguing with Frank, who would insist Jim join him for dinner.

That damn pride again.

Before he left Jim to his new post, the officer unfurled the scarf from around his neck and handed it to the old man. "Here, now. If you're gonna be stubborn, at least be stubborn and warm all at once."

These people were really trying to wear him down. They won't even let a man be curmudgeonly anymore, Jim thought, stifling a smile while trying his hardest not to look as overwhelmed by the officer's kindness as his heart wanted him to. A simple thank you would have to suffice, and it took everything Jim had to accept it without tears or resistance.

He was a man who once reveled in gifts of silk and satin, the finest goods the world had to offer and the most expensive that money could buy. But holding that wool scarf between his cold, aching fingers, Jim truly thought it was the greatest Christmas gift he'd ever received.

The feeling of that scarf around his neck was a comfort the likes of which Jim hadn't known in a long time. Perhaps it was how soft and warm it was. Or maybe it was all the walking. It could have been listening to O'Malley all that time. Whatever it was, it was hard to fight; and with a yawn, he closed his eyes to the morning light. The cold faded away as he felt nothing but the calm, dark peace of sleep.

CHAPTER 5

THE MAN OF GOD

O come, all ye faithful
Joyful and triumphant
O come ye, o come ye to Bethlehem

The bear-like growls of Jim's snoring were audible well before Father Anthony even set foot onto the block. In any other instance, Anthony's large, black shoes would have sounded like horses clomping through downtown. Today they were drowned out by the overpowering noise of this old man, firmly in the arms of Morpheus.

Father Anthony looked at Jim and smiled, reciting under his breath:

"And Jesus said to him, 'Foxes have holes, and birds of the air have nests, but the Son of Man has nowhere to lay his head.'"

Raising his index and middle finger, the holy man made the sign of the cross, whispering a blessing that would have been hard to hear under normal circumstances, let alone over the snores of slumbering Jim. He knelt long enough to slip a few coins into Jim's pocket and stood up as Mrs. Wallace passed by across the street, young Henry in tow.

"Merry Christmas Eve, Father!" she happily shouted with a broad wave. Henry was visibly less enthused about being on the way to the grocer.

"And a Merry Christmas Eve to you!" the young priest greeted her in return with a wave, his smile changing to uncertainty as she passed. He looked down at Jim once again before cupping his gloved hands together for a rub of warmth and then pushing the door open into the barber shop.

Frank was just pulling the apron away from Officer O'Malley, seated in the chair looking dapper with a fresh new trim. If the Lord above had blessed anyone with the gift of gab, it was O'Malley, and as always, the officer was not afraid to put his gift to use.

"...I mean all's I want is to see my sister and nieces and nephews for Christmas," O'Malley finished telling

Frank as Father Anthony entered. "With our folks gone, they're the only family I've got. And they're a hundred miles away. But with everybody else in the department off fightin,' I'm the youngest guy on duty. All those old-timers are taking the day off, but I'm low man on the totem pole. Oh, hey, Father."

Anthony hung his long black coat on the rack in the corner and took a seat near the front window just on the other side of Jim's stifled snoring.

"How are we today, Officer?" Anthony asked with a smile.

The boisterousness with which O'Malley seemed to speak often reminded Anthony of many an exuberant young choir boy at St. John's.

"Dandy, Father. Dandy," the officer replied. "I was just talkin' to Frank here about...naw, no need to bother *both* of you gentlemen with it."

O'Malley looked himself over in the mirror, admiring both his neatly trimmed hair and the way he looked once his uniform cap was again firmly on his head. He conspicuously and awkwardly leaned over the priest to glance at the sidewalk below the front window.

"How's Jim doin' out there, Father? Had a bit of a rough time this morning with Mr. Flanagan, the old grouch."

Anthony pursed his lips as he thought for a moment. "Whoever closes his ear to the cry of the poor will himself call out and not be answered."

O'Malley stood blankly for a moment, then smiled, hoping no one had noticed his lack of comprehension.

"Hey, that's pretty good, Father."

"Well, I wish I could take credit for it, my boy. Proverbs 21:13."

The officer shrugged and cheerfully pulled 35 cents out of his pocket, handing it over to Frank for services rendered.

"Well, hey, if he wakes up soon, tell Jim I said 'bye,' will ya? Merry Christmas, Frank. I'll see you tonight, Father. Lookin' forward to that Christmas Eve sermon!"

Like a bull released from its corral, O'Malley buoyantly exited the shop and continued on his patrol. His rendition of "Jingle Bells" failed to wake Jim from his slumber but continued to boom for several blocks before fading into the distance.

No sooner had Father Anthony taken his place in the chair than the apron twirled through the air with a whoosh, landing gently around the young priest. He watched as the barber's hand quickly shook like a machine, tossing away the water droplets from the comb.

"So, what's tonight's sermon gonna be, Father?" Frank asked as he smoothly ran the comb through Father Anthony's hair.

"You want the truth, Frank?"

"I'd want nothing less from you, Father."

Anthony sighed. "I have no idea. I haven't come up with it yet."

The snip-snip of the scissors filled the ensuing silence. Frank had yet to respond, continuing to work away at Anthony's hair with all the focus and attention of a battlefield surgeon.

"Hard to find the right words at times," Anthony continued. "Especially these times."

"I thought last week's sermon was wonderful," Frank said assuredly, looking down his nose with a squint as he prepared for his next move across Anthony's head.

"Well, thank you, Frank. I appreciate that. But talking about offering kind words to each other was easy."

A quick turn of the barber's wrist and the water was flowing freely from the sink. He ran the comb under the water, shaking off any excess hair as he weighed in.

"I would think Christmas must come pretty easy, Father."

His palms anxiously pressed together as if in prayer, Father Anthony let out his frustrations with another loud sigh.

"I stand up at that pulpit, telling people that God is watching over us, that his goodness shines through us all. I get up there and preach about love and the blessedness of life. Then I read the news and if it's not more of the boys over there getting killed, it's someone's home catching fire, or someone getting killed right here at home."

The scissors hovered, awaiting a suitable moment to continue, as Frank's gaze moved slowly from the priest's hair to his face; the young man's internal turmoil on full display. His hands separating, Father Anthony gestured to punctuate every syllable of unrest as he spoke.

"How can I... how can I continue to convince others that the Lord is watching over us when each day I... I guess I question it myself?"

Frank resumed trimming, moving from one side of Anthony's head to the other, surveying the sideburns, but not saying a word. The young priest seemed far from finished, and Frank knew better than to interrupt the flow of someone's soul-searching merely to hear himself talk. So, he continued with a snip here, a snip there, his ears open to the rhetorical pleas from this man of God.

"I used to believe we lived in a world full of good people, Frank. But there's just so much hate out there. And for what? Nothing that matters. You can have so much in common with your fellow man, but you're supposed to hate him, why? Because of skin color? Because of his religion?"

Frank tilted his head, his eyes growing a little wider, accepting the statement without comment and letting Father Anthony continue.

"Is the family next door who you wave to every morning, who mows the lawn beside you every Saturday, who helps you shovel the sidewalk and just...lives so much like you do in so many respects, going to burn in Hell because on Sunday they head to a different church than you do? We're all supposed to be children of God, aren't we?"

Frank nodded silently but with clear approval. The priest's animated hands moved about as if he was telling a story rather than airing internal grievances.

"Are we really to believe that it matters to those sitting side by side in the trenches which God they pray to at night?" Anthony asked. "As if...as if a direct hit meant the man to your left was bound for paradise while the one on your right was headed to eternal damnation?"

Anthony continued to talk; the barber's ritual snipping seemed to clear away the clutter from inside the priest's head as it shaped the outside.

"Archbishop Spellman in New York told troops that in serving the country for a just cause, they're also serving God. An archbishop in Detroit wrote President Roosevelt talking about patriotism guided by Christian virtues, promising the bishops would marshal the spiritual forces at our command to keep safe our God-given freedom. But who's free, Frank? Who's really free? You? Me? Is little Benjamin standing in the cold with his shoeshine box really free? Is Hiram from the jewelry store really free? What about all those Italian folks who were put into camps in Maryland and Texas and those other places? Most of 'em were only let out in September. Or the Japanese? We're still putting them into camps. Is that free, Frank? Or have we just convinced ourselves that we should be grateful for what our leaders give us and shut up about it?"

"I thought we were talking about God," Frank said, a slight smile brightening his face.

Father Anthony stammered a bit, his hands motioning as if they were tossing a ball back and forth.

"I am. I mean, how can you look around at all of this in the world and believe the Lord is out there somewhere looking out for you, let alone convince your parishioners of it? It just...it doesn't seem right, Frank. Sometimes I feel like a phony."

"You probably shouldn't say that during your homily," Frank said, amused at the thought of such brutal honesty coming from the pulpit at Christmas Eve mass.

"Are you kidding? They'd excommunicate me." Father Anthony's chest expanded as if he had breathed in all the air the room had to offer, slowly exhaling in a heavy sigh that seemed to indicate no solution in sight for his plight.

"War can make even a nonbeliever fall to his knees and pray for spiritual comfort. So why has it started to make me question everything instead?" Anthony wondered aloud. "It seems we're losing more boys every day..."

Anthony's eyes caught a glimpse of John's warm gaze staring from the photo beside the mirror and it gave him pause.

"I'm...I'm sorry, Frank. I didn't mean to..."

Frank said nothing, his eyes turned downward to the top of Anthony's head, surveying his handiwork, and letting him continue.

Anthony could feel Frank's breath on the back of his neck. He had talked for so long he never even stopped to hear what the barber had to say.

Frank sighed. "Honestly, Father? I don't think it's so much what we believe as much as believing in *something*. What it is isn't nearly as important as whether or not it gives us hope."

He spun Anthony around in the chair, until the two were finally looking at each other face to face instead of through the reflection of the mirror. His tools now set aside, Frank's right arm lay across his torso, his left arm resting upon it as the hand supported his chin. He looked a bit like a philosopher in a white coat as he carried on.

"In the end, it may not matter who's right and who's wrong about it," Frank told him. "I think for many folks, it's about having something or someone to look to for hope. Sometimes hope is the most powerful thing a human being can have. Sometimes it's what we need more than anything. It motivates us, it inspires us, it leads us to believe that anything can be possible, that tomorrow can be better than today. Some of us find that hope in God. Kids find it in Santa Claus or Superman. We find it in a spouse...or a..."

Anthony could see Frank's eyes drift toward the photo of John.

"...or a... a child..." Frank's voice faded and cracked. He turned away for a moment, his back turned to Father Anthony so that all could be heard was the sniffling nose and swallow of a man composing himself. When he turned back around, he was dabbing his nose with a handkerchief that was then quickly stashed away in his pocket.

"In a world as uncertain as this, Father, isn't hope really what we need above all else?"

Father Anthony stared at him as he gazed to a faraway place.

"Hope...huh..."

Within a few moments, his previously sullen lips turned upward and opened, until his bright white teeth displayed the smile that had greeted many a parishioner.

"God bless you, Frank."

Grabbing his hat and coat, Anthony handed Frank an excessive pile of coins, closing them up in

Frank's palm before the barber could see how much he had been overpaid. The priest rushed from the shop as if a fire was near. Indeed, there was, but it was a cerebral and soulful flame that had ignited Anthony's spirit. His excitement and inspiration could hardly be contained, and he shouted to Frank through the window as he exited, hurrying toward to the church.

"And Merry Christmas!"

CHAPTER 6

THE RADIO KID

Bring your coats and hats

You lukewarm cats

I've got my horn to keep me warm

"Just a little off the top, Frank."

Neal hopped into the chair with all the energy and enthusiasm of a child, which in many ways he still was. A bow tie sat neatly wrapped around his neck, his sweater vest drooped over his scrawny frame not unlike that of a scarecrow.

"Big night tonight?" Frank asked, reaching for the scissors.

"Ho! Ho! Ho!" Neal bellowed. "You're looking at a guy as jolly as Santa Claus, my friend! Tonight Jack says his on-air farewell and announces his replacement on the show."

"I'm guessing from the way you're about to leap out of that chair and through the ceiling, it's gonna be you?" Frank asked.

"From your lips to God's ears, Frank old boy!"

Neal was a ticking time bomb of energy ready to go off at periodic cycles. He reminded Frank of Andy Hardy from those Mickey Rooney movies, only Neal probably would've been much better off with James and Emily Hardy for parents than the ones he had. His decision to chase stardom on the radio didn't sit well with Neal's folks; and from the day he had made his choice, he'd been on his own.

He was the biggest star on the airwaves...or so he liked to tell everyone he met.

It was a passion that harkened back to that one day in high school. There Neal was, sitting in the audience with his classmates as Betty Griffin broadcast one of her original youth radio programs on WIBX using kids from area schools as the on-air talent. From the moment he saw the way the crowd reacted to his peers in front of the microphone, Neal was hooked. He had been bitten by the showbiz bug, and there was seemingly no going back.

Even the after-school job he had as a teen, making deliveries for Garro Drugs, was orchestrated so he'd have a reason to visit the WIBX studios. Up he would dash to the ninth floor of the First National Bank building downtown with an order of Bromo to settle the stomachs of frazzled directors or licorice laces and soda pop for the talent. Neal found any reason he could to hang around and try to be 'part of the gang.'

Whether it was pity on the kid for how hard he tried or being worn down by his persistence, the walking gabfest that was Neal landed himself a low-tier spot among the players of the WIBX Dramatic Guild every week.

He'd been second, or more accurately fourth, banana alongside crooners, comedians and actors for several years since, never giving up on the idea that he was skyrocketing up the ladder of fame. For a regional radio station, Frank found them all to be pretty good, but to Neal, they were everything - entertainers, artists, stars...and acceptance.

Neal talked a big game, but Frank saw through his bluster. Behind it was a loneliness that would never be satiated by career movement.

"Any Christmas plans, Neal?"

"Show goes on the air at eight, live and loud to radios everywhere! That's all the holiday I need right there."

"Gonna stop by and see your folks?" Frank asked.

"Aw, nuts to them!" Neal said dismissively, waving his hand through the air. "They can turn the dial to 1230 and hear me on the radio any time they want. *If* they want. And after tonight, I'll be on a whole lot more once I'm named the star of the show. I might even give up my gig driving the cab, things are looking so very merry!"

"So that's it?" Frank prodded. "That's Christmas then?"

Neal's face quickly turned red as his defensiveness took over. "Well it sure beats sittin' in my apartment with a can of beans looking at the lights of downtown, now don't it?"

Neal paused as Frank continued to snip.

"But you know, there really is something beautiful about them, isn't there, Frank?"

"What's that?" Frank asked for clarification.

"The lights downtown," Neal explained. "Starting at Genesee and running as far as the eye can see. The lights on the marquee of the Stanley, the wreaths hanging from the lamp posts. It gives a fella a good feelin' inside, you know?"

"So, with this cast shake-up…" Frank segued. "If they name you the lead of the show tonight…"

"*When*, dear Frank. *When*," Neal cut him off, a correcting finger pointed upward like a schoolteacher.

Frank chuckled but tried to hide it. "Right. *When* they make you the lead. Then what?"

"Well whattaya mean?!"

Neal's temper was starting to flare again, but Frank remained unfazed, ever the unflappable barber.

"What I mean," Frank began. "is what comes next?"

Neal's eyes lit up like a pair of twinkling Christmas lights as he thought about the possible future awaiting him. "More shows, more parts, more money, more women - oh boy!"

Rubbing his hands together, Neal was like a kid sitting at a banquet table before a veritable Christmas feast, even if that feast hadn't quite happened and only existed in his mind.

"So that's it then?" Frank asked. "Your life mission accomplished? You've got a lot of years ahead of ya to have nothing else to aspire to."

"Aw, what do you know?!" Neal retorted.

Frank's bottom lip went up as he shrugged and ran Neal's brown locks through his fingers to measure and level the cut. "Eh, you're probably right, Neal. What do I know?"

For a few moments, the only audible sound was the snips of Frank's scissors and "In the Blue of the Evening" on the radio. By the time Sinatra finished crooning, Frank broke the silence. "Did you catch *The Shadow* on Sunday night?"

"Boy, did I! That was something, wasn't it?" Neal exclaimed with an exuberance that made Frank pull back the scissors for fear the young man would leap clear out of the chair and get punctured. "*The Club of Doom*! Wowee! Health Club members murdered! Only Lamont Cranston can crack the case! Y'see, Frank.

That's why you'll never catch me in one of those health clubs."

Frank smiled as Neal continued.

"Now *there's* the kinda show I wanna do, Frank. I mean, the *All-Star Cavalcade* is great and all. Tonight I get to play Scrooge in this Christmas Carol routine, right? It's hilarious. But *The Shadow*! Oh boy! Mystery! Adventure! That's the stuff I was made for. What a gig that Bret Morrison's got, huh?"

"You know," Frank chimed in. "It used to be that young man from the Mercury Theatre who was The Shadow a few years ago, Orson Welles. Then came Bill Johnstone, then Morrison."

"Boy, you're better than the Hollywood columns, Frank. Maybe you should be workin' in radio," Neal said, quickly raising a finger up into the air. "Just don't horn in on my territory, my good man. Honor among gentlemen and all that."

Frank smiled.

"Well, y'know, those entertainment magazines over there don't just keep the customers occupied. I've gotta have something to read between my clients. And don't worry. I wouldn't dream of interfering with your stardom, Neal."

"Darn tootin'," the youth smiled into the mirror, displaying a perfect ham in the reflection. "Say, with a revolvin' door of actors like that, who knows? Maybe *I* could be The Shadow one day!"

Frank shrugged. "Eh, who knows what the future holds?"

The two men looked at each other and smiled, both in on the joke, raising their hands and waving their fingers in the air.

"The Shadow knows!" they shouted in unison before rolling into different heights of laughter.

As he tried to compose himself, Neal wiped a tear of joy from his eye and continued to look for some more common ground with the old man.

"Whatcha think of Jack Benny this week?" Neal asked, eager to keep the conversation about radio going.

"By that point, I was taking my Sunday walk and I missed it," Frank admitted.

"Aw, it was good," Neal said with a grin. "Jack and Mary went Christmas shopping."

"Mary's back, huh? Seems like she's been out the past few shows."

"Laryngitis," Neal responded, acting as if he had insider information rather than the very public announcement made on the airwaves.

"Oh," said Frank, running his scissors under the cold water of the sink.

"Yeah. S'why I gotta keep myself in tiptop shape, Frank. Can't let the fans down, y'know?"

"Of course," Frank said, brushing a few hairs from Neal's shoulders and spinning the boy around in the chair to get a better look at his handiwork.

"Ya hear Gene's headin' off to war?" Neal asked him.

"The one on the air with you over at the Guild?" Frank asked. "I did not."

"Yeah," Neal said with a sigh. "Tonight's his big sendoff. Between that and Jack headin' out to Hollywood, our director's gonna be *livin'* off his Bromo. Of course, it, uh, certainly helps *this* young lad's chances at movin' up the cast ladder."

Frank stared off, his mind adrift at the thought of another young man putting himself in daily danger for the sake of all of those back home. A near-whisper escaped his lips: "I hope he stays safe."

"Jack's a grown man, Frank. Hollywood can't knock him down," Neal said, dismissing any concern before realizing Frank was not referring to Jack. "Oh. You mean Gene. Yeah. I told him not to rush into things, but nope, he was dead set on it."

"What made you not want to enlist, Neal?"

"Me? Well, don't get me wrong, Frank, I love the good ol' U-S of A as much as anybody, but…"

Neal paused, obviously thinking about the answer to a question he had never actually been asked before. It took him a few moments before he could put his thoughts into words.

"Well, why's everybody gotta go over there to help out, Frank? There's stuff back here needs doin' too, ya know. Blackout drills, scrap drives…and well…amusement. If everybody was shipped over there, there'd be nobody left on the radio, or the stage, or the screen to remind those guys what they're fighting for."

"You're a regular Bob Hope, Neal."

"Oh, hey, speakin' of which, he and Bing Crosby got a special show on tonight, right after the *Cavalcade*. Glad I can warm the audience up for those guys," he said with a boyish smirk that could have indicated a joke, but the twinkle in his eye showed that he actually believed it himself.

"Saw you walking out of the Colonial last week with Peggy Wilson, Neal," Frank observed with a raised eyebrow, like a baseball pitcher waiting for the young man to take the swing.

"Well, what can I say? There's still a lot of lonely women back here on the home front, my dear Frank, and most of 'em are looking for a little company," Neal said, his eyebrows bobbing up and down as a big smile lit his face. He adjusted his bowtie in the mirror while he admired himself.

While Frank saw a hometown version of Andy Hardy, it was obvious Neal saw Casanova looking back at himself in the reflection.

"I'd be careful" Frank warned. "That's Christopher Powell's girl, isn't it? Don't think he'd take too kindly to that when he gets back."

"Aw, phooey!" Neal retorted. "He's halfway around the world, probably romancin' some girl in France or somethin' as we speak. 'Sides, Peggy asked *me*! She's a grown, independent woman! She can make her own decisions, can't she? Said she sent him a Dear John letter last month."

"How very modern," Frank said dryly, rubbing a dab of hair oil through Neal's locks for a little shine.

The booming sound of bells from the steeple of Grace Church rang in the distance, throwing Neal into a sudden spasm. He pushed up the left arm of his tweed jacket to expose the watch underneath, frantically tapping it when he saw the hands had frozen at noon. Sliding down the barber chair and out from under the skilled hand of Frank and his scissors, Neal ran around Frank's shop like a canine under the influence of a dog whistle, stopping once he found the small clock Frank kept on a shelf. Neal grabbed it, held it close, stopping to count the bell tolls ringing through the air before looking back at the small clock to confirm his fears.

"Five o'clock?!" he shouted in a panic. "If I don't get to the studio for run through, I'm a dead man! Or worse, they'll write me outta the show!"

Neal's fists clenched as he struggled to get his coat on, tripping over himself and stumbling out the door. "Why didn't ya tell me, Frank? Whattaya, tryin' to ruin my career?!"

Frank concealed a smile as he watched Neal slip and slide down the sidewalk in his hurry to catch the trolley to the station.

Looks like I won't be getting paid for that kid's cut 'til next month, he thought. *Maybe.*

CHAPTER 7

THE GIRL

Should auld acquaintance be forgot
and never brought to mind?
Should auld acquaintance be forgot
and days of auld lang syne?

In Jim's mind, scant seconds had passed since he let himself fall asleep outside the barber shop, but as he rubbed his eyes, the world came into focus and he realized that night had fallen, as had the temperatures. Ribbons on Christmas wreaths glittered against the light of the street lamps above. Officer O'Malley was long gone, and with a now empty shop on Christmas Eve, Frank was dressed in his overcoat, leaning against the icy-cold building exterior just a few feet from where Jim was sitting on the frigid sidewalk.

"The President's gonna be on the radio in a bit, Jim. If you want to come inside and listen..." Frank said, feeling out if the old codger was going to let the spirit of Christmas take his guard down this time.

"Love that man, but hate this war," Jim said. "Besides, if I come in it's only a matter of time before you start trying to get me to eat with you. And I don't care what you say, nobody wants to have dinner with a washed-up vagabond like me."

"At this point in life, Jim, I've learned there's no point in arguing with you."

Frank reached into his pocket, pulling out two paper bills, handing them to Jim with the kind of subtlety reserved for spies in the pulps.

"The Imperial's got a Christmas dinner with all the trimmings for a buck twenty-five. Sounds mighty good," Frank said as his breath turned into to a visible cloud as it collided with the cold night air.

"I'm not taking that. I don't want your charity, Frank."

Frank bent his knees, squatting on the sidewalk so that he was level with Jim.

"It's not charity, Jim."

"What is it, then?"

"A Christmas present."

"It's not like I have anything to give you in return," Jim grunted.

"Sure you do," Frank said. "Promise me to stop inside the shop once a week or so with some good stories."

"Stories?"

"Oh, I don't care when they're from," Frank told him. "Today, yesterday, twenty years ago. But I know you've got them locked up in there, Jim. And I want to hear 'em."

"Why?"

Frank shrugged his shoulders, "I just like a good story. And as far as storytellers go, you're up there with the best of them."

His palms placed firmly on his knees, Frank pushed himself upright once again, the bell above the shop door ringing as he opened it to go back inside. Before he did, he turned one more time to Jim. "Merry Christmas, you stubborn old mule."

Jim looked at the two dollars in his hand. He hadn't held that much money between his fingers in some time. On a night devoted to the king of kings, Jim felt like royalty himself at the moment. He turned to the barber, his voice cracking.

"Merry Christmas, Frank."

Jim smiled as he rose from the frosty sidewalk and made his way down the block, whistling "Jingle Bells" until those familiar notes faded into the distance.

As Frank moved from the icy surface of the sidewalk to the slightly less chilly linoleum floor inside, he realized he had forgotten to turn the radio off, its sounds echoing through the shop's nighttime emptiness. *The All-Star Cavalcade* presented by the WIBX Dramatic Guild was in full swing, and Jack had just finished crooning a tune that would have been marginally better it they weren't being sung as a duet alongside a gallon of bourbon. Jack said his goodbyes to the cast and the audience, making a much bigger deal of himself than anyone else would. *You'd think he was leaving the planet, let alone a radio broadcast*, Frank thought to himself. *But that's what happens when you believe your own hype and orchestrate your own send off, I suppose.*

Jack spent so much time talking about himself and the shiny future he thought was waiting for him out west that Frank wondered if they'd still be on the air by the time he got around to announcing his replacement. And with a build up like that, Frank, though far away from the halls of the radio studio, could feel the proverbial punch to the gut Neal took when it was young Mary who was named as the *Cavalcade's* new star following Jack's exit.

I'm never getting paid for that kid's haircut, he thought.

Frank shook his head and reached for the radio dial, giving it a quarter turn to the right until the static slowly took the form of a mellifluous but familiar voice - Lionel Barrymore.

Ordinarily, Frank preferred the silent solitude of the shop as the evening stretched on, but tonight...tonight there was something different in the air. Perhaps tonight wasn't the kind of night to be alone with one's thoughts, or at least not with Frank's thoughts.

"...but tonight I'm not going to play the part of Scrooge..." Barrymore boomed through the speaker. *"Let me rather take you people of America by the hand at the side of your loved ones fighting in every corner of the globe. Our president, commander-in-chief is with us, too. He'll speak to our armed*

forces and then he has a word for us, as well. We're going to Italy, North Africa, New Guinea, Guadalcanal, New Caledonia, yes and for the first time on the radio, we'll take you to Munda. We'll visit China, where it already is Christmas. We'll go to India, Panama, Alaska, Pearl Harbor, and some of our ships of the Navy. Yes, in this, our third year of war, we Americans are going to spend Christmas Eve at the fighting front with our men as they light up Christmas trees all over the world."

"Do you think he's there?"

Her voice was smooth, like the kind of silk many couldn't afford even before the war. The words read Frank's mind and the voice stopped him in his tracks. Bing Crosby and Bob Hope were said to be coming up shortly, but he wouldn't hear a word of what came after Barrymore's opening greeting, no matter how long it continued to play through the small speaker in the background. Frank turned to see Myrna in what was perhaps the finest green dress ever made.

"No," he said, almost inaudibly.

"Well that's a fine how-do-you-do," she replied, perching casually in the same chair where the likes of Officer O'Malley, Father Anthony, and even that pesky radio kid had sat just hours before.

"You asked a question, I answered," Frank said calmly. "No. I don't think he's there."

She was tall compared to most of the women Frank knew. She was certainly taller than he, but then, in all honesty, that wasn't saying much. His stock came from a region not exactly known for producing giants. Seated in the barber chair, though, she seemed a little less towering, at least in physical stature. Her larger-than-life spirit shined through no matter where she stood, no matter the crowd or company. She was right at home on the stage of the Little Theatre outside of town behind Remington Arms. Before that, it was the Players of Utica until tough times cost them their home in the old New Hartford Movie Theater.

"Well, I'm not giving up hope, and neither is my letter-writing hand," she told him, bluntly. "Whattaya say to dinner, Frank? Christmas Eve dinner, you and me? I just got out of rehearsal and I'm starving."

"Rehearsal on Christmas Eve? Is nothing sacred anymore?" Frank said half-jokingly.

"The director's a maniac," she replied, eyeing the empty shop. "Though if you want to throw stones...a barber staying open late on Christmas Eve with no customers?"

He said nothing—but gave up a smile.

"It's a charity performance for the Salvation Army," she said, grasping the clasp on her handbag, opening it and reaching in. She pulled out two pieces of paper that she presented to him with little ceremony. "Here. If you decide to come. I'm playing Elvira, the ghost ex-wife of the main character."

"*Two* tickets?" he asked, puzzled as he adjusted his glasses to read the small print on them regarding showtimes. "You want me to see a show *and* make a friend to take too? You're asking a lot, Myrna."

She tilted her head, her lips pursed in a wry half smile, his self-deprecating humor nothing new to her. "Take Ms. McCallister from the school. She'd love to go with you."

"Pfh," he said, waving his hands through the air, dismissing the subject entirely.

How much she's grown, Frank thought. *How in the world was the young woman sitting in that chair the same little girl who would play with John down the sidewalks of the neighborhood? Hopscotch in the street, boxcar races, school dances.* It all seemed like a lifetime ago. But then, for many of them, it was.

Frank remembered Myrna crying as much as he did the day John left. Somewhere along the line, her tears had become as infrequent as her visits to the house, dried up behind the bright smile, magnetic charisma, and determined soul that made her a natural on stage and a joy to be around.

He had all but forgotten how much fun the three of them had had together, playing cards on the front porch and laughing into the early morning hours. The joy she and John brought to a room when they were together kept Frank from falling into the darkness after Barbara passed just shy of their 30th anniversary.

Like coming out of a dream, Frank shook away the memories and the pale joy they brought back with them. Silence filled the air until he took several steps to the sink, saying nothing in the process.

"Well, I guess I should go," she said, grabbing her wool coat from the rack. "If you change your mind about dinner…"

Frank was fumbling with some scissors and a brush, running them under water from the same faucet that he already cleaned them in several times over since the last customer of the day. He was less than convincing in his urgency and need to look away.

"Sure. Sure. If I do, I'll let you know," he replied.

She held the door to the shop open with one hand, while the other fussed with the buttons on the double-breasted coat. The stylish wide shoulders made Myrna look broader than she actually was, but no less beautiful, and her cocked hat gave her a movie star quality. She stood in the open doorway as if an invisible force blocked her movement, letting the chill invade the room. The light from the lamppost out on the street crept through, bathing her in an eerie yellow glow as she turned.

"I miss him too, you know," she said, her hand falling to her side, letting the door shut again.

The clang of the metal instruments hitting the sink as they fell from Frank's hands echoed like a cavern amid the silence.

"I know," he sighed quietly. "I know."

Her hat and coat still firmly in place, she approached him slowly, like a wanderer through the forest not wanting to spook a deer.

"And I get it. Or at least I think I do. Me being around just reminds you of him. I get it. But at the same time, it leaves me with nobody too, Frank. And I hate it. I absolutely hate it. You're like my dad...only fifty times better than he could have ever hoped to be. Having you in my life was everything I didn't have at home. It was amazing. We were a family." She paused. "A real family."

Frank said nothing, although she thought she saw a tiny smile form along the right side of his mouth, but in the dim light, it was hard to tell.

"I thought the hardest thing I'd ever have to do was let John go when he signed up. I can't imagine what that was like for you as his father. I'm sure it felt the same way. But at least there was some comfort that while he was gone, we had each other."

Like the cowboy standoffs in an Old West movie, the two figures stood several feet apart. Still, the distance seemed closer than either had felt those past several months.

"When the letters stopped, when we heard nothing for so long...that's when I needed you the most, Frank. And you wanted nothing to do with me.

I needed family. You needed family. And all we gave each other were cordial and civil hellos instead of anything that would make the pain a little easier to deal with."

She swept a finger under her eye, wiping clear the tears that were forming around the rim. "You sit here all day and talk to everyone else with a smile on your face and a song in your heart, but when we cross paths, it's so obvious how much it pains you to even look at me."

"He was my son," Frank said quietly, his head hanging low, obscured by darkness unreachable by the lights above.

"And he's my fiancé," she shot back at him. "We were a family. Now it's like we're strangers, Frank. And it tears me apart."

His brow furrowed as he slammed his fist on the table next to the sink, the jolt causing scissors, razors and blades to jump.

"You think I'm not?" he shouted. "He was my son! You're...you've been like my daughter since you were knee-high, and now...now I'm supposed to just look at you and not think of him every time you come by?"

"We can't keep ignoring it, Frank. John would want us to…" She didn't get a chance to finish before Frank's voice boomed in a way few had ever heard.

"He's gone, Myrna! Gone! Why don't you see that?!"

She said nothing, just staring at him, tears running down her silent face, which only made Frank stumble more. His voice began to crack, and his voice quickly turned to a hushed, almost ashamed whisper as he repeated himself.

"Why don't you…see that?"

She sniffed, her mouth open, but a few seconds passed before any words came out.

"Because I have hope," she whispered, wiping the remaining tears from her cheek. "I have to have hope."

They stood there not saying a word to each other for what felt like hours, but was little more than a minute. The only sounds were the humor and harmonies that came from the radio just a few feet away. There was no winner here. There couldn't be.

"I'm gonna go," she said, sniffling again. "If you change your mind about dinner...well, let me know. Otherwise, I'll be spending Christmas Eve with Dick Powell."

Frank blinked to make sure he heard her correctly. When she knew she had his attention, she continued. "Last showing of *Riding High* with him and Dorothy Lamour over at the Stanley. Sure, I'll be a little late, it already started, but it's...it's better than nothing. Merry Christmas, Frank."

She turned, and walked out the door into the street light's glow before disappearing into the dark of the distance. Frank fell into his chair, face to face with his own visage in the mirror. He spent so much time looking at the top of people's heads and their hairlines in that piece of glass all day he rarely spent time paying attention to himself. The face looking back at him was more wrinkled than he remembered, the eyes more sunken and heavier, like a burden that couldn't be shaken. He turned his head to look out the window, but it was too late. She was gone. Looking back at himself in the mirror, he closed his eyes and did something he had not allowed himself to do. He wept.

CHAPTER 8

THE PRODIGAL SON

I'll be home for Christmas
You can plan on me
Please have snow and mistletoe
And presents on the tree

"*O*n this Christmas Eve there are over 10,000,000 men in the armed forces of the United States alone. One year ago, 1,700,000 were serving overseas. Today, this figure has been more than doubled to 3,800,000 on duty overseas. By next July 1 that number overseas will rise to over 5,000,000 men and women.

That this is truly a world war was demonstrated to me when arrangements were being made with our overseas broadcasting agencies for the time to speak today to our soldiers, *sailors, Marines, and Merchant Seamen in every part of the world."*

As the President's voice emanated from the radio, it was accompanied by a chorus of squeaks from Frank's rag pressing up and down against the mirror. He put a little extra force behind the wiping when it came to the mirror in order to make sure he cleared away any stray remnants of Brylcreem that always seemed to mysteriously make their way to its slick surface. He had scolded more than one apprentice over the years for not wiping it regularly and leaving a film of the beeswax, mineral oil and water substance at the workstation.

"In the Southwest Pacific, in Australia, in China and Burma and India, it is already Christmas Day. So we can correctly say that at this moment, in those Far Eastern parts where Americans are fighting, today is tomorrow. But everywhere throughout the world - throughout this war that covers the world - there is a special spirit that has warmed our hearts since our earliest childhood - a spirit that brings us close to our homes, our families, our friends and neighbors; the Christmas spirit of 'peace on earth, good will toward men.' It is an unquenchable spirit."

Frank had no goodwill for the stubborn strands of hair on the linoleum floor that seemed to stick like bubblegum, taunting both barber and broom as he went over the same spots time and again - under the chair, under the workstation, in the back room, until a pile of hair, enough for a wig, seemed to materialize at his feet. All the years of cutting it and he was still amazed at where and with how much speed hair could travel once it hit the ground. With a few more sweeps of the broom, it all went into the dustpan and the floor itself now seemed clean enough to eat Christmas dinner from, not that Frank wanted to test that theory.

"During the past years of international gangsterism and brutal aggression in Europe and in Asia, our Christmas celebrations have been darkened with apprehension for the future. We have said 'Merry Christmas—Happy New Year,' but we have known in our hearts that the clouds which have hung over our world have prevented us from saying it with full sincerity and conviction. And even this year, we still have much to face in the way of further suffering, and sacrifice, and personal tragedy. Our men, who have been through the fierce battles in the Solomons, the Gilberts, Tunisia, and Italy know, from their own experience

and knowledge of modern war, that many bigger and costlier battles are still to be fought."

Every brush, comb and scissors got its moment under the faucet, rubbed and scrubbed and released from the remnants of the day's work, ready to start anew. The skin on Frank's hands felt dry and tight as he wiped them with a towel, which then joined its brothers waiting in the laundry pile.

His brow furrowed as he carefully took a mental inventory of pomades, oils, powders and soaps at his disposal before breathing a sigh so loudly it could have been heard uptown. Pulling on his coat, he straightened the collar and looked around for his hat. He hoped it hadn't accidentally gone home with a client again. It took him three weeks to get it back that time Neal thought it was one of his props. His eyes darted around until zeroing in on the radio. With the hat resting atop, its dials and speaker made it look just like a cartoonish face. One with the voice of the President of the United States, no less.

"But—on Christmas Eve this year—I can say to you that at last we may look forward into the future with real,

substantial confidence that, however great the cost, "peace on earth, good will toward men" can be and will be realized --"

The Commander-in-Chief was abruptly silenced with the turn of a dial. As Frank pulled the old wool coat over his arms, he stopped for a moment, clutching Barbara's photo in his hands.

"I wish I knew," he quietly said to the picture, as if expecting a reply. "I wish I knew what to think, how to be. You always knew."

He paused a moment when he found that his voice was cracking.

"You always knew," he repeated. "Merry Christmas, my love."

Reverently returning the photo to its customary place, Frank put the hat snugly on his head and turned off the lights until little could be seen of the shop minus the reflection of street lamps in the mirror. With a turn of the hand, he locked the door tight and put foot to pavement, the squeaking of his shoes drowned out by the whistle of the cold wind and the cacophony of sound summoning parishioners to Christmas Eve Mass. As the barber headed homeward, the President's unmistakable baritone emanated faintly from radios in houses all along the way; some loud and clear, others barely audible.

"Some of our men overseas are now spending their third Christmas far from home. To them and to all others overseas or soon to go overseas, I can give assurance that it is the purpose of their government to win this war and to bring them home at the earliest possible time. We here in the United States had better be sure that when our soldiers and sailors do come home they will find an America in which they are given full opportunities for education, and rehabilitation, social security, and employment and business enterprise under the free American system—and that they will find a Government which, by their votes as American citizens, they have had a full share in electing."

Roosevelt's words began to fade as the sound of church bells grew nearer, the beautiful steeple coming into view. A cab rounded the corner up ahead, nearly taking out a lamppost as it hurried off with a pair of last-minute shoppers in the back, clutching their wrapped packages as if their lives depended on it, which, with Neal behind the wheel, was quite possibly the case. Frank was glad to see that even if radio stardom had eluded the young lad once again, he was still making ends meet by putting passengers and pedestrians in jeopardy.

Frank was nearly plowed over by a tower of boxes in the arms of a behemoth heading his way and taking up the entire sidewalk. Jumping aside just in time, he was somehow not surprised to see it was Officer O'Malley on the other side of the precariously stacked Christmas presents, hurrying down the sidewalk with little time to pause.

"Sorry 'bout that, Frank!" the officer shouted as he rushed past. "Sister surprised me by bringing the family to see *me*! 'Course, I had to get somethin' for the kids! Merry Christmas, Frank!"

He passed the brick exterior of Grace Church where the doors were propped open to the usual overflow Christmas Eve crowd. He heard the bells of St. John's echo in the distance, and he pictured Father Anthony delivering his sermon to a reverent congregation.

Through the cold night air, he trudged, deviating from his usual path and making his way to Oriskany Street so he could peek in on old Whistlin' Jim. As he passed the Imperial Restaurant, there was Jim, seated by the window, laughing it up with fellow diners as if they were old friends, the steam rising from a plate of hot food in front of him, and a smile on the faces of all those around him.

A block or two beyond the restaurant, the sound of footsteps grew louder. Frank suddenly realized they had been there for quite some time but were difficult to distinguish amid all the commotion of downtown. As Frank's own steps slowed, so did those of the stranger. As Frank walked faster, so did whomever was following.

"Christmas Eve is a heckuva night to try and rob an old man," Frank muttered as he turned to face whatever fate had in store for him. His eyes noticed the simple, mundane fact that snow had begun to come down like white confetti all over the city. When those eyes focused on his mystery follower, Frank froze.

It was John. *His* John. All 6 foot 2 of him. He looked tired, weary, but there was no mistaking that smile. It was his mother's smile, set under a nose so much like Frank's own, it was distinguishable anywhere.

Frank didn't ask how. He didn't ask why. He knew there'd be plenty of time for that in the time to come. There was nothing else that mattered in that moment but the open embrace of father and son, as the two hugged tight, tears running down their faces, filled with so much relief that they could burst.

All those minutes, hours, days and months had led to this. The unspoken feelings of that time apart magnified the moment. All the worry, fear, unknown, disbelief, anger, sadness, denial, defeat, depression, mixed with a hundred more indescribable emotions, washed away by joyful tears.

The heart-filling moments of life had ceased to exist. Memories of holding a bundle of joy and first steps, A's on exams and hours shared at the barbershop had been paused, ready to be erased upon receipt of the awful news Frank had expected. Instead, he could breathe fully for the first time since John signed his life away. They could continue the record where the song was left off. The gift of a family moving onward; a gift so many others were missing out on. The two men knew of their luck and cherished it.

Santa was not needed. At least not here, not this night. Both men got what they wanted for Christmas. A gift of a lifetime that could never be beat.

The End

SONG INDEX

Irving Berlin. Performed by Bing Crosby. "White Christmas," Decca Records, 1942.

Michael Carr, Tommie Connor, and Jimmy Leach. Performed by Vera Lynn. "The Little Boy That Santa Claus Forgot." 1937.

Leon Jessel and Ballard MacDonald. "The Parade of the Wooden Soldiers." 1922.

Franz Xaver Gruber and Joseph Mohr. "Silent Night." 1818.

Frances Wade. "O Come, All Ye Faithful." 1751.

James L. Pierpont. Performed by Glenn Miller and His Orchestra with Tex Beneke, Marion Hutton, Ernie Caceres, and the Modernaires. "Jingle Bells," RCA Victor, 1941.

Robert Burns. Performed by Guy Lombardo and His Royal Canadians. "Auld Lang Syne," Decca Records, 1939.

Kim Gannon and Walter Kent. Performed by Bing Crosby with John Scott Trotter and his Orchestra. "I'll Be Home for Christmas," Decca Records, 1944.

Christmas Eve in Utica, New York 1943

While the tales of Frank and his customers are fictional, they take place in the very real world of Utica, New York, which in 1943 was a city bustling with people and activity. The snippets to follow are, in contrast to Frank, quite real, and hopefully add a bit more color to Utica the week of Christmas, 1943.

Rhoads General Hospital

Like many parts of the city of Utica, Rhoads General Hospital was busy the week of Christmas 1943 preparing for the upcoming holiday. Rhoads was helped in their efforts through the generosity of the Utica community, exemplified by the 25 foot Christmas tree donated by Utica Unit 229, American Legion Auxiliary. Decked by volunteers with tinsel, lights and ornament, the tree added a festive welcome to the Red Cross auditorium at the hospital as soldiers gathered there on Christmas Day. Aside from the sight of delightful tree trimmings, patients and enlisted men at the hospital were bestowed with more than 2,500 festively boxed gifts, courtesy of various organizations and individuals within the community. The Central Garden Committee, which included 10 local garden clubs, worked together in decorating table and mess halls for the Christmas dinner at the hospital and making center table arrangements. One of the clubs decorated matchboxes for cigarettes to accompany favors.

Located on Burrstone Road at a site now housing Notre Dame Jr./Sr High School, the Utica Business Park, and the Elihu Root Army Reserve Center, the 100+ building facility was named for Army surgeon Col. Thomas Leidy Rhoads. According to the New Hartford Historical Society, Rhoads was an active Army post for patients in need of rehabilitation and convalescent care, arriving via special medical trains that came behind the hospital itself. The Rhoads site housed its own post office, phone center, theater, laundry facilities, bakery, sewing shop, chapel, quarters for nurses, barber shop, Red Cross building, and much more.

Rhoads General Hospital served more than 25,000 patients from through 1946 when the hospital closed, all its land and buildings declared to be war surplus and sold by the government.

Source: New Hartford Historical Society, Utica Daily Press, Observer-Dispatch

Penny Shortage

Banks in the city of Utica were publicly advertising their need for thousands of dollars' worth of pennies. Local bankers felt that if they could convince people to put their pennies in circulation, they could get the minimum $8,000 in pennies they and other banking institutions needed.

The Oneida National Bank took out ads in the Utica Daily Press and the Observer-Dispatch asking citizens to get their pennies back into circulation. Oneida National President Charles W. Heil suggested that anyone with pennies should spend them or take them to the bank to exchange for silver or bills, declaring them too important and that they must be kept in circulation.

Source: Utica Daily Press

Sled and Papers Stolen

A 12-year-old newspaper carrier named Dominick put his sled to good use during Utica's winter season, sliding his heavy bundles of the Daily Press and Observer-Dispatch over snow and ice as he made deliveries. The Tuesday before Christmas, one might have wondered just where the spirit of the season was hiding as Dominick made a delivery inside a store on Jay Street, only to come out and find his sled, newspaper bag, and newspapers gone. The determined newsboy continued on his route that week, carrying the heavy bundle of newspapers over his shoulder.

Source: Utica Daily Press

A Family Affair

Some families said goodbye to sons or fathers in service to the WWII cause, but for the Schremphs of Sylvan Beach, it was a family affair. The Observer-Dispatch on behalf of Oneida County saluted the Schremph family the week of Christmas, noting that the entire family - father, son, and step-mother, were all enlisting in the Navy. The family patriarch, Jacob, was noted by the newspaper as an experienced Barge Canal tugboat captain. Their 17-year-old son headed to Sampson Naval Training Base, while mother began training at Hunter College as a WAVE (Women Accepted for Volunteer Emergency Service).

Source: Observer-Dispatch

Old-Fashioned Dance

Faculty and students of the School of Art at Munson-Williams-Proctor Institute danced the night away in period garb to the sounds of Frank Tobin's orchestra at an old-fashioned country Christmas party held in the exhibition room of the Institute. The evening awarded two attendees for their old-fashioned costumes - Mrs. Eva T. Geer for "most typical garb of the Gay '90s" and Arthur Rosenblum for "the most representative farmer."

Source: Observer-Dispatch

(Most) War Plants get Christmas Off

Employees at all war plants in the Utica area were given the holiday off to spend time with their families. The War and Navy Departments encouraged this wherever possible within the war industries. The single exception to this was Skenandoa Rayon Corporation on Broad Street in Utica.

Built in 1882 to spin cotton yarn for local textile manufacturers, the mill was converted to the production of rayon in 1926 for use in the production of clothing items.

Due the production processes requiring 24-hour operation, it was necessary for the plant to stay open, though only half of the plant's employees had to work the holiday, according to management at the time.

Source: Observer-Dispatch, Oneida County History Center

Holiday Cards from Schoolchildren

Students of all ages rang in the season at Seymour School with a series of holiday events that included music, recitations, and a second grade play called "The Toys Find Christmas." Sixth graders presented a gift of five dollars to the USO (United Service Organizations). The school also sent out Christmas cards to more than 75 former pupils who were serving with the armed forces.

Source: Observer-Dispatch

Under the Christmas Tree

For the fourth consecutive year, employees and officers of the First Bank & Trust Company, along with members of the community, donated toys for children in need. Placed under the foot of a Christmas tree in the bank lobby, the toys, for children ages 5-14, were distributed to four Utica institutions - the contagion pavilion of the General Hospital at South and Mohawk Streets, St. John's Orphan Home adjoining St. John's Catholic Church on John Street, the Children's Hospital Home which was an outgrowth of the Utica Orphan Asylum, and the House of the Good Shepherd.

Source: Observer-Dispatch

Scrap Metal for the War Effort

The city of Utica exceeded its goals for scrap metal collection in the last quarter of 1943 and did so by a whopping 266,742 pounds! Just in the month of December alone, the Utica community collected 2,704,796 pounds of iron and steel toward the war effort.

Through the recycling of unwanted or unused metal, the U.S. government was able to build airplanes, ships, and other equipment needed to fight the war.

Source: Observer-Dispatch

Paper Profit-Sharing

Utica Daily Press and Observer-Dispatch Publisher J. David Hogue announced that employees of the newspaper would share 15 percent of the company's profits for 1943. How much each employee received was based upon their individual earnings over the previous five years and would go to all employees who had been employed with the papers for a full year. The papers' employees who were serving in the armed forces would also participate in the profit sharing. The action, in line with that of the papers' parent company, Gannett, was not new. The company said that it distributed the funds for years on a basis of 10 percent of the profits, but as in 1941 and 1942, the board of directors voted to increase that by an extra five percent in recognition of higher living costs.

Source: Observer-Dispatch

1943 Cost of Living

Average Cost of new house - $3,600.00
Average wages per year - $2,000.00
New Car - $900.00
Cost of a gallon of Gas - 15 cents
Average Rent - $40.00 per month
Bottle Coca Cola - 5 cents
Average Price for a new car - $900.00
Army Doctor/Nurses Kit - $1.98
World War II Model Plane Kits - $1.00 for five
World War II Plane Models - From 23 cents
Tuition to Harvard University - $420 a year
Movie Ticket - 35 cents
First-Class Postage Stamp - 15 cents
Ground Coffee - 46 cents per pound
Granulated Sugar - 75 cents for 10 pounds
Bacon - 45 cents per pound
Eggs - 21 cents per dozen
Hamburger - 30 cents per pound
Fresh Baked Bread - 10 cents per loaf
Milk - 62 cents per gallon

Source: The People History, History Daily

On the Big Screen

The Highest Grossing Films of 1943

This is the Army - Warner Bros.
For Whom the Bell Tolls - Paramount Pictures
The Song of Bernadette - 20th Century Fox
Stage Door Canteen - United Artists
Thousands Cheer - Metro-Goldwyn-Mayer
Casablanca - Warner Bros.
Coney Island - 20th Century Fox
Destination Tokyo - Warner Bros.
Dixie - Paramount Picture
So Proudly We Hail - Paramount Pictures

Top Ten Money-Making Stars of 1943

Betty Grable
Bob Hope
Bud Abbott and Lou Costello
Bing Crosby
Gary Cooper
Greer Garson
Humphrey Bogart
James Cagney
Mickey Rooney
Clark Gable

The Spinner Rack

Some of the many four-color comic books on newsstands in December 1943

Action Comics #69
Batman #21
Black Terror #5
Captain Marvel Adventures #31
Fighting Yank #7
Flash Comics #50
Green Lantern #10
Marvel Mystery Comics #52
Miss Fury #3
National Comics #40
Police Comics #27
Smash Comics #50
Superman #27
Walt Disney's Comics & Stories #40

Source: Mike's Amazing World

The following World War II-era posters were issued at the time by various U.S. government agencies, representing the government's effort through art, illustration and photographs in an effort to unite the American people in a time of adversity.

These posters come courtesy of Northwestern University Libraries.

For Liberty and Peace on Earth

Give WAR BONDS

GIVE WAR BONDS ★

★

The Present with a FUTURE

"KEEP 'EM FLYING"

IS OUR BATTLE CRY!

FIRST CLASS FIGHTING MEN NEEDED

AVIATION CADETS . . . . .
Young Men, 18 to 26 Years
of Age Inclusive, for Air Crew
Training as Bombardiers,
Navigators and Pilots.

SOLDIERS . . . . Aggressive,
Alert, Patriotic, Young Men,
18 and 19 Years of Age, Who
Want to Fight for Their
Country, Especially Desired.

APPLY TODAY AT ANY U. S. ARMY RECRUITING STATION

They've got more important places to go than you!...
Save Rubber
CHECK YOUR TIRES NOW

ABOUT THE AUTHOR

DAVE DELLECESE has authored a variety of novels, children's books, comics, and graphic novels, occasionally blogging about life and parenthood as The Dorky Daddy. A former journalist and news anchor, he currently lives in Central New York with his wife, children, and cats.

davedellecese.com

CPSIA information can be obtained
at www.ICGtesting.com
Printed in the USA
LVHW110254021220
673196LV00021B/148

9 781970 156003